W9-CPV-658

# Freddy!
## DEEP-SPACE FOOD FIGHTER

# Freddy!
## DEEP-SPACE FOOD FIGHTER

Written and Illustrated by

## PETER HANNAN

**HARPER**
*An Imprint of HarperCollinsPublishers*

Library of Congress Cataloging-in-Publication Data
Hannan, Peter.
  Freddy, deep-space food fighter / written and illustrated by
Peter Hannan. — 1st ed.
    p.  cm.
  Summary: Human boy Freddy, king of the planet Flurb
and its out-of-this-world characters—including his
scheming sister, Babette—finds himself the target of some
interplanetary threats.
  ISBN 978-0-06-128468-7
  [1. Human-alien encounters—Fiction. 2. Brothers and
sisters—Fiction. 3. Family life—Fiction. 4. Kings, queens,
rulers, etc.—Fiction. 5. Humorous stories.] I. Title.
PZ7.H1978Fp 2011                          2010019298
[Fic]—dc22                                      CIP
                                                 AC

Typography by Alison Klapthor
11  12  13  14  15   CG/CW   10 9 8 7 6 5 4 3 2 1

First Edition

For Todd and Liz

# ★ CONTENTS ★

# FLURBIAN JOYRIDE

A bright orange blur streaked and looped across the purple Flurbian sky. It took a sharp downward turn and then shot straight up again. Screaming and yelling rang out across the multicolored landscape, but it quickly turned into laughter . . . uncontrollable laughter.

It was King Freddy and Glyzix riding Orange Beauty on a high-speed tour of the Flurbian wilderness. Freddy's crown flew off his head, and Glyzix immediately replaced it with another. It was the eleventh crown Freddy had lost that afternoon, but it was totally worth it.

Now the seven Flurbian suns were about to set. "We'd better head home, Kingster," said Glyzix. "On Flurb, when the suns go down—"

"I know, I know," said Freddy. "They go down *fast*." As if on cue, the suns suddenly dropped like stones beyond the far hills, plunging Flurb into total darkness.

Just as suddenly, Orange Beauty turned downward in a wild death plunge.

"AHHHHHH!" yelled Freddy.

"C'mon, O.B."—Glyzix yawned—"you're going to scare our young ruler out of his wits."

Orange Beauty's eyeball lit up like a headlight. The ground was closer than Freddy thought.

"AHHHHH *AGAIN*!" he yelled.

But just when it looked like they were about to be flattened on the rocky Flurbian surface, the ground opened up and they plunged into one of Flurb's many underground canals. Freddy closed his mouth and held his breath as they went deep into the water, but before he knew it, they popped back up to the surface and were all laughing again. The canal twisted and turned and dipped and dropped like the wildest water park ride in the universe. What a planet.

# A HEAVY MESSAGE

By the time Freddy and Glyzix slid down Orange Beauty's tail, the whole palace was asleep. Not just the residents—the palace *itself* was asleep . . . and snoring.

"Good night, Kingster," said Glyzix, shaking blue sand from his head plumes. Then he yawned, scrunched inside himself, and blasted off like a spring-loaded rocket to his room.

Freddy entered the royal sleeping chambers and looked over at his bed, which was gigantic, bigger than his entire house on Earth. In fact, it was so big he had created a bed within a bed that became his cozy, private getaway. The mattress was covered with all Freddy's stuff—gadgets, comic books, leftover birthday cake. His birthday had been a couple of days ago. Everyone in the kingdom had given him amazing presents—stuff he couldn't have even imagined back on Earth. And his parents had given Freddy the only thing they had. It was a tiny flashlight that Dad had grabbed off his nightstand when they were being abducted. It said JOE'S HARDWARE on it, and, though it wasn't much, it was Freddy's favorite gift. Mostly because it was from his parents and it reminded him of home. Babette, on the other hand, hadn't given him anything. "I'll give you a birthday present when you get me off this stupid planet," she'd said.

Freddy brushed his teeth and washed his face (actually, his personal-hygiene robot did it for him). Then he took off across the floor toward the hovering Flurbian-style trampoline that he used to jump onto the bed. He was in midair when he heard it—a high-pitched whine that sounded like an incoming missile. Freddy immediately tucked and rolled and slid *under* the bed for protection, just as a large meteorite crashed through the arched bedroom ceiling, through Freddy's bed—slicing off the points of Freddy's crown as it passed—and through the floor. Freddy heard a gigantic crash down below, and then the low, rumbling voice of the palace said one word: "Ouch." Freddy looked down the hole and saw that the boulder had blown through four more floors on the way to its final resting place in Orange Beauty's stall, located directly below his room. The gigantic green rock had landed right on the royal steed's tail, but it hadn't woken her up. Orange Beauty could sleep through anything.

Everybody else was jolted awake though and Freddy's mom was the first to enter his bedroom. She saw the gaping hole and imagined the worst.

"MY FREDDY! MY ADORABLE LITTLE FREDDY, KING OF FLURB!"

"I'm okay, Mom," replied Freddy from under the bed, but she couldn't hear him over her own screaming.

"DISASTER! WOE IS ME! WOE IS *FLURB*!"

Babette shuffled in and put her hand over her mother's mouth. "I have a feeling your

precious little brat king may have survived this incident," she said.

"How do you know?" Mom asked between sobs.

"Because I can see him under the bed, which is exactly eighteen times the size of my whole bed*room*, by the way."

"How can you think of bed size at a time like this?" said Mom.

"Uh, guys," said Freddy, wriggling out from under the bed. "Huge hole here."

Freddy led the way and everyone followed him down to the stables. Wizbad was already there, and he had found a large envelope tied to the boulder.

"Well," said Wizbad, "what have-est we here?"

"It look-eth like-eth a rock-eth and an envelope-eth," mocked Freddy. He loved to make fun of the way Wizbad spoke. He knew it wasn't very nice, but Wizbad wasn't very nice either. He was basically an evil, greedy, all-around pain in the nergzip.

"Very amusing-eth," said Wizbad, trying to hide the fact that he hated Freddy more than anything in the universe. Literally. More than *anything*. Once he had gotten a splinter in his eye from a Flurbian fire-spice tree, and even that hadn't bothered him half as much as Freddy. He blamed Freddy for everything, including his broken fang. It caused him excruciating pain—but Wizbad refused to get it repaired because he *liked* being reminded of his hate for Freddy. He was just that nuts.

Still, Wizbad had to be very careful not to make his real feelings known. First, because the Flurbian people absolutely adored Freddy. And, second, because Ex-King Wormola (now enjoying his retirement . . .

fishing for space trout, playing space bingo, whatever) had chosen Freddy as his replacement and was watching from afar, keeping an eye on the diabolical wizard.

Wizbad opened the envelope. He pulled out a handheld scanner translator and read the message:

"'Greetings, Freddy, King of Flurb—

"'Welcome to the neighborhood. We, the undersigned, hate you. The attached rock is a symbol of that hate. We hoped it would land on you and squash you, but if you're reading this, it obviously didn't, so we'd like to take this opportunity to say (and please scream as loudly as possible when you read this):

"'GET OUT OF THE GALAXY AND TAKE YOUR LAME-O FAMILY WITH YOU! . . . OR FACE OUR WRATH, EARTH DORK!'"

11

"AHHHHHHHHHHHHH!" screamed
Mom, Dad, and Babette.

"But wait-eth, there's more," said
Wizbad.

"'And by "wrath" we mean the immediate invasion of Flurb and a public pulverizing of you and your family and the rest of the population with the brand-new industrial-sized pulverizer we just ordered from a catalog. It was a pretty good deal—we split the cost three ways.

"'Sincerely yours—'"

"Well, at least they're *sincere*," interrupted Freddy, "because if there's one thing I can't tolerate, it's insincere, bloodthirsty neighbors."

"SILENCE-ETH!" screamed Wizbad, before he caught himself. "Heh-heh. What I meant-eth to say was *please,* let me finish, your highness. Eth."

"Oh, all right," said Freddy.

"'Sincerely yours,

"'Chewtyke, Supreme Leader of Molaria

"'Big Bad Wongo, *Supreme-er* Leader of Wongolia

"'Deathsnail, *Supreme-est* Leader of Z-9X G-Vector.'"

"Catchy name for a planet," said Freddy.

"Freddy!" screeched Babette. "Being pulverized would seriously cramp my style, once we get off this stupid planet. By the way . . . do you know what time it is?"

"No," said Mom.

"IT'S TIME FOR US TO GET THE HECK OFF THIS STUPID PLANET!" screamed Babette.

# THERE'S NO BADNESS LIKE WIZBADNESS LIKE NO BADNESS I KNOW

Five minutes later, the evil Wizbad was in his chambers, laughing it up with the Venomoids, his three cyborg hench-snakes.

"They fell-eth for it!" Wizbad laughed. "They art so-eth stupid."

"More like *you* is so *smart!*" Twork giggled.

"You's a genius!" Babs screamed.

Blif was laughing the hardest of all. "I's also a genius too!"

Wizbad looked at Blif in disgust. "The only reason I don't turn-eth you into space urchin soup again is that I'm in too good-eth a mood."

"Good" was not really accurate. "Evil," "vicious," and "dastardly" were more like it.

"Twork, could you explain it again to the brainless wonder here?"

"Sure, boss." Twork looked at Blif and spoke slowly. "Freddy and all those other stupids thinks

the leaders from those planets chucked that space rock and wrote that note."

"But they *did*, you stupid!" said Blif.

"No! *I* hurled the rock and *I* wrote the note!" screamed Wizbad, smoke curling from his ears. "It is all part of my plan to take the crown from the Freddy!"

"Boss!" said Blif. "If all you wants is a crown, I gotted one in my King Dress-up Play Set you could have." Wizbad couldn't take it anymore. He leaned his head wand toward Blif and zapped him with just enough wizard juice to paralyze his tiny brain for a few hours. The Venomoid's face was frozen in a moronic smile.

"I don't want-eth some stupid toy crown!" said Wizbad. "I want-eth to be king of Flurb, and this time I have a foolproof plan. Everyone thinks that the most powerful leaders of the galaxy hate the Freddy, and if the Flurbians are convinced that having the Freddy as a leader puts them in danger, they'll find-eth their lovable king a lot less lovable. And then we move into phase-eth two of my operation: we make the foreign leaders *actually* hate-eth the Freddy—even more than *I* do."

"Yippee!" squealed Babs.

Wizbad rolled his eyes. "That was a joke!" he shrieked. "No one could possibly hate-eth the Freddy more than I do!"

# GUESS WHAT'S COMING TO DINNER

Freddy and company discussed the threatening message in the royal breakfast nook the next morning.

"All I'm saying," said Babette, "is that if these murderous dictators want us to leave, I say we leave. Immediately!"

"I agree," said Dad. "Not being pulverized on Earth *is* much better than being pulverized on Flurb."

"Silence, Royal Boot Polisher!" said Glyzix.

"Please, my name is Al!" said Dad.

"Silence, Royal Boot Polisher named Al!" said Glyzix, just to make Dad mad.

"Freddy, snookums," said Mom, "what do *you* say?"

"I say we invite these alien creeps over to the palace. Once they get to know me, they *have* to like me."

"Don't bet on it," said Babette.

"Maybe we should throw a fancy dinner party!" said Mom.

"A dinner party? Like suits and ties and being so bored you want to curl up and die? Stuff like that?" asked Freddy.

"You want your mother to be proud, don't you?" said Mom. She stuck out her lower lip and tilted her eyebrows into a sad expression, then pretended to wipe a tear from her eye.

"Oh . . . all right," Freddy said. "Glyzix! Alert the Royal Inviters! Wait . . . do I *have* Royal Inviters?"

"Of course you do!" said Glyzix. "You have royal everything. In fact, the Royal Inviters have already sent out the royal invitations and the Royal RSVP Getters are on royal alert."

"How royal of them," said Freddy.

# WHAT'S ALL THE HUBBUB, BUB?

For the rest of the morning, servants raced around, preparing the palace for the big event and Freddy and his family found getting through the hallways was like strolling down the middle of a freeway at rush hour. The Flurbians did what they could to avoid crashing into Freddy, and that meant crashing into everyone else . . . but mostly Babette.

"Watch it!" she screamed the fifth or sixth time she got plowed into.

Flurbians were scrubbing the floors, walls, and ceilings so fast, it caused a tidal wave of water and detergent to wash through the hallways.

Glyzix and Freddy hopped onto a hover chair that cruised along above the foam.

Freddy's family was not so lucky. They were swept away by the current.

"Glyzix," said Freddy, "we've got to help them!"

"Don't worry," said Glyzix. "They need to be cleaned and groomed for the dungeon anyway."

"Dungeon?!" screamed the family.

"Just kidding! I mean for *dinner*!" Glyzix laughed.

"I'm not sure they appreciate your sense of humor," said Freddy.

# BLOODTHIRSTY, YES, BUT SPOILED BRATS TOO

Freddy and Glyzix wound their way through the palace on their hover chair.

"Let's check in on the RSVP Getters," said Freddy, leaning hard to the right.

The chair took a sharp turn and headed straight for a wall, but the wall quickly opened and they zipped right through the mouthlike hole.

When they got to the RSVP-getting room, the Flurbians inside looked concerned.

"Big problem, King Freddy!" sang three Flurbian ladies. "Deathsnail refuses to sit next to Big Bad Wongo, who refuses to sit next to Chewtyke, who refuses to sit next to anyone. They agree on only one thing: they hate one another."

"Well, they actually agree on two things," said Freddy. "They hate me too. No matter! Let's get them on the interplanetary communicator. I'll use the old Freddy charm."

"Absolute genius!" sang the three RSVP Getters.

"So royal!"

"So regal!"

"So king-ish!"

# HATE AT FIRST SIGHT

"Communication Chamber descend!" shrieked Glyzix.

A huge bell-shaped chamber floated down from the ceiling, covering Freddy and Glyzix. Glyzix punched a bunch of numbers on a keypad, then the chamber flickered, and holograms of the three ugly alien leaders appeared.

Chewtyke was a tiny but terrifying little

space troll. His lips didn't move when he spoke. He just growled and ground his razor-sharp teeth, making an irritating metal-on-metal scraping sound.

Big Bad Wongo's large, reptilian noggin had six faces, and they were all horrible. Each of his mouths was drooling, slurping, and spitting. Some of his eyes were on the ends of spines sprouting from the top of his head. He didn't have legs—just one wheel instead.

Deathsnail was the creepiest. Snails on Earth are known for their incredible slowness, but Deathsnail was anything but slow. He twitched in sharp, spastic movements, speaking incredibly fast, like he'd had *way* too much coffee. Deathsnail was brimming with violence, and it seemed like he would much rather eat you than say hello. His bloodred pupils glowed inside dirty yellow eyes.

The leaders were all speaking, but Freddy had no idea what they were saying. "Glyzix, how am I supposed to charm them if we can't even understand one another?"

"Simple, your highness," said Glyzix.

"The communicator is equipped with a translator."

"Sweet," said Freddy.

Glyzix flipped dozens of switches. "All right, Kingster, you're good to go. Everyone will understand everyone now."

"Okay," said Freddy. He gathered his thoughts. He had to think of something to say that would make them hate one another less, which seemed highly unlikely, and not hate *him*, which seemed highly *impossible*. He'd give it his best shot. "Greetings, Chewtyke, Big Bad Wongo, and Deathsnail!" he said. "Let me say how honored I am to meet you all. I am confident that we can all be buddies. Maybe watch movies, play video games—you know . . . hang out! I can't wait to shake your hands . . . or whatever you have that you like to shake!"

There. They couldn't possibly find anything in that statement to get mad about. The control panel of the communication chamber blinked and beeped, while Freddy waited for the translations to be delivered into the ears of the alien leaders.

There was a long pause as the dictators listened carefully to the message. Suddenly, all three snapped their heads back. Their faces turned several shades of purple and contorted into horrible expressions. They each opened their mouths very wide—in Wongo's case, six mouths—and then they screamed at such a high pitch that the entire communication chamber exploded into thousands of pieces. The three Flurbian RSVP Getters leaped high in the air and embedded their nails deep into the ceiling like terrified cats.

"Well," said Glyzix, "that went well."

The fractured chamber lay shattered on the floor. In every piece Freddy could see tiny holographic images of the angry alien leaders. Amazingly, the badly damaged control panel still seemed to be working. It blinked for a while, and then finally translated the screaming message into Freddy's ears.

"Due to the horrible things you just said,

we've decided to put aside our hate for one another so we can concentrate on hating you. However, we accept your invitation to dinner. We will bring our royal chefs and share our favorite meals . . . and, if all goes well, you have a chance of not getting pulverized. It's a very slim chance though."

# THE GREAT MISCOMMUNICATOR

Back in Wizbad's chamber, he and the Venomoids were watching all this in the wizard stone. They were laughing like lunatics because Wizbad had messed with the communication chamber. He had reprogrammed it to turn everything Freddy said into the worst possible insults—really bad things about how the aliens' mothers were incredibly ugly and

their feet stank. Stuff like that.

"I am so-est wonderful," said Wizbad, "and by wonderful, I mean-eth wonderfully evil."

# BEAUTY IS IN THE COUNTLESS EYES OF THE BEHOLDER

Babette, Dad, and Mom, having recovered from being swept away by the sudsy tidal wave, were in the middle of a beautification process in the royal dressing chamber. The room had come to life—literally. Hoses spewed enormous quantities of suds and lotions, and robotic arms came out from the walls and washed and brushed the startled family. They all got poked in the

ribs and tickled way beyond the point of enjoyment.

Babette was especially ticklish on the bottom of her left foot, and the robotic fingers went right for that spot. At first, Babette laughed so hard she cried . . . and then she just plain old cried.

But soon the scrubbing phase was complete and then came the dressing. Each family member rose off the floor and

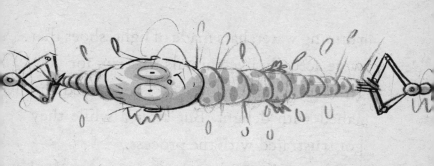

hovered helplessly in midair in front of a large white screen, wondering what would come next.

As they were floating there, three Flurbian beauty technicians came in and sat at a long table, facing the family. Using joysticks, they ran through a variety of outfit changes and looks for each family member. They seemed to have access to fashions from across the universe and made changes at incredible speed.

Long hair, short hair, striped hair, checked hair, rainbow hair. Dresses made of running water, hats made of light, shoes that were actually live animals that *run* for you. At first the family loved it. They oohed and aahed with delight. But after a while they got frustrated with the process.

"I saw what I wanted about two hundred looks ago!" said Babette.

"Well, it's not really up to you, boot licker," said a technician who looked like a cross between an ugly lizard and an uglier coyote. "*We* are the beauty experts around here."

# 10

# VICIOUS VISITORS
# INCOMING!

It was almost time for the guests to arrive. The grand entranceway to the palace had been decorated by the Flurbian servants in preparation for the party. Gigantic, superflattering, and completely inaccurate portraits of the alien leaders were painted on banners in the courtyard, where Freddy stood, waiting.

Soon, three piercing notes rang out

across the city, signaling their arrival. Tall clouds quickly formed, turning the sky dark purple and then black. Freddy thought it would be best to ride out to meet the aliens, so he summoned Orange Beauty, who promptly arrived and lowered her escalator tail for Freddy. He rode it up, hopped aboard, and hollered, "GIZZABOOTLE, GIZZABOOTLE, GOINK, GOINK, GOINK!" at the top of his lungs.

Orange Beauty whinnied and took off like a turbocharged racehorse—and in about two seconds they reached the three incoming ships.

"Greetings!" said Freddy. But the ships just blew by him. Orange Beauty did a quick U-turn and followed them down. The ships were headed for the planet's surface at an alarming speed, and it looked like they were going to crash, but Freddy had finally gotten used to this kind of thing on Flurb. He knew the ground would open up at the last second, allowing the three ships to safely plunge into the underground canal.

Wrong. The ships crashed into the blue Flurbian dirt and exploded in flames.

"That's gotta hurt," said Freddy.

# 11

# DISPLEASED TO MEET YOU

By the time Orange Beauty and Freddy landed softly nearby, the smoke had cleared and Chewtyke, Big Bad Wongo, Deathsnail, their weird team of assistants, and their chefs emerged from the wreckage totally unharmed. Actually, the top of Chewtyke's head was on fire, but Freddy didn't know if that was from the crash or if it was always on fire.

Chewtyke calmly reached up and cupped
the flame with his hand, snuffing it out like
a candle.

Glyzix passed Freddy a handheld translator. "I had the boys in research and develop-
ment whip it together. This should work a
lot better than the communication chamber,
boss."

"Thanks, Glyz," said Freddy. He confi-
dently approached the alien leaders.

Wizbad stood in the doorway, laughing

to himself. Then he tipped his head wand in the direction of the translator, distorting the sound waves and garbling Freddy's words.

"Greetings to you all!" said Freddy.

Deathsnail, Chewtyke, and Big Bad Wongo waited for the translation . . . and then growled like rabid dogs.

Freddy turned to Glyzix. "What's their problem *now*?" he asked.

Glyzix shrugged. Maybe this wasn't the time for small talk.

The good news was that the leaders actually *had* brought along their personal chefs, so perhaps there was still a possibility of sharing a meal . . . and avoiding a war.

"Follow me," said Freddy, and the whole freaky procession made its way through the palace gate. Deathsnail left a very smelly trail of slime, and Big Bad Wongo's wheel spun in it, spraying the disgusting substance

onto the others. Chewtyke reacted by growling and grinding his teeth some more. Following the leaders were weird assistants followed by weird chefs carrying weird utensils. It was weird.

Freddy was a bit nervous about what these strange cooks might come up with, and he thought maybe his mother could help them out and keep them from whipping up anything too disgusting. "Let's go inside and meet my family," he said into the translator. "They will be happy to assist you in the kitchen!"

The alien leaders growled again. Now they also foamed at the mouth.

# DEADLY MIX-UP

**M**om, Dad, and Babette were lined up inside the doorway of the grand hall of Flurbishness, ready to meet the alien leaders. The Flurbian beauty technicians had certainly worked their magic. Mom looked like some kind of strange bird. Dad looked like a hairy potato. Babette looked like a moldy pile of garbage.

"Hi, Freddy," Mom said cheerfully. "What

do you think of my makeover?"

Freddy tried to say something truthful but not insulting. "Mom . . . you look *unbelievable*. In fact, I don't believe it." He looked at his father and sister. "You *all* look unbelievable."

Babette looked unbelievably *unhappy*. But the alien leaders gazed upon her like she was a ravishing beauty, which made her feel a bit better.

Freddy spoke into the translator: "Meet my wonderful family. . . ."

"Ooooooo," said the alien chefs, looking positively overjoyed.

"I'm so glad you're hitting it off," said Freddy. "Why don't you go get started!"

The chefs nodded and smiled in approval as Flurbian guards led them and the family down the hall.

"Thank goodness!" said Babette. "This whole garbage thing simply isn't working for me."

"I'm not big on this weird bird look either," said Mom.

"I don't even *like* potatoes," snarled Dad. "Especially hairy ones."

All three of them wanted to get remade over so badly, they jumped to the false conclusion that the chefs were another crew of beauticians. Freddy, of course, knew they were chefs, but forgot that his family *didn't* know. Since he thought that his words were translated correctly this time, he assumed that the aliens were simply happy to have the family help out in the kitchen. And, of course, the chefs thought a third thing. Instead of "wonderful family," they had heard "delicious ingredients."

Wizbad was amused.

# PET PEEVE

"Okay, then," said Freddy, turning to Deathsnail, Chewtyke, and Big Bad Wongo, Wizbad, and the Venomoids, "follow me!" They all entered the dining room.

Just then, there was an enormous whimper, whine, and crash right behind them and Orange Beauty's huge eyeball bulged through the doorway. She forced her way in, demolishing the wall in the process, and spun across the recently polished floor like a gigantic hippo sliding across ice. She scrambled to her feet and panted with her tongue hanging out like a ten-ton puppy.

"Isn't she the cutest?" said Freddy into the translator. "She wants to dine with us."

But the alien leaders hissed and screamed and shook their heads, as if Orange Beauty, the gentlest creature in the universe, was some kind of horrible monster. Chewtyke's head burst into flames again.

All of Big Bad Wongo's mouths roared. Deathsnail started twitching uncontrollably and it seemed like his eyes would pop out of his head. Freddy realized that it might be a mistake to let Orange Beauty stay.

He approached her and spoke in the language they had devised. He hopped on one foot and wiggled the other while snapping his fingers and whistling. He flapped his arms, made a series of sounds that really cannot be described, and then stopped.

Orange Beauty didn't take what Freddy said seriously and just rolled over on her back like she wanted to have her massive belly rubbed. Freddy had to get tough with her. He whistled one incredibly loud note that said it all: "TO THE STABLE! *NOW!*"

Orange Beauty's face fell. Literally. It fell onto the floor. The entire palace shook. She looked up again and revealed the saddest

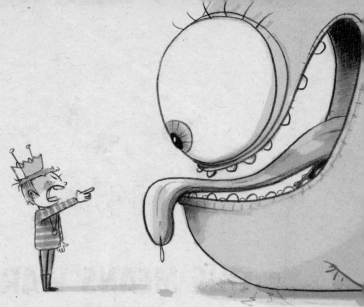

expression Freddy had
ever seen on any creature anywhere. He
felt terrible, but there was nothing he could
do. Freddy stomped his foot and pointed
skyward. Orange Beauty tilted back and
flapped her wings. But it wasn't her usual
joyful takeoff. This time, she stuck her tail
between her legs and cried like a baby as she
shot through the skylight. Her tears fell like
rain upon the alien leaders, which ticked
them off even more.

# THIS MEANS WAR

Freddy shrugged his shoulders and made an expression that meant *Sorry about that.*

Freddy, Glyzix, the alien leaders, their assistants, Wizbad, and the Venomoids all took their seats around the dinner table. Deathsnail's assistant looked like a snail without a shell. He was covered with slime and had trouble sitting upright. Chewtyke's assistant had two grotesque mouths where his eyes should be. His actual eye was in the normal nose position and a handlike thingy jutted from his chin. Strangest of all, Big Bad Wongo's assistant looked like an Earth female. Except she didn't have a body—just a head and neck with four tiny arms sticking out.

Little sliding doors opened in the tabletop in front of each diner, and plates of squirming appetizers appeared. Next, goblets of boiling blue beverages rose on mechanical platforms. Something was swimming in them.

"Well," said Freddy, speaking into the translator and trying not to be sick, "I can't tell you how happy I am that all of you could come." He lifted his glass and shouted, "To all of us!"

"To all of us!" shouted Glyzix.

"GRAAAAAAAAAAAAAAAGGG!" shouted Deathsnail.

Freddy looked at the translator nervously. Translation: "DIE!"

Wizbad almost laughed out loud but caught himself.

"O-*kay*," said Freddy. This was going to be one long night. He decided to try to lighten things up. "Glyz, perhaps you could entertain our guests a bit?"

Glyzix immediately leaped on top of the table and started juggling his eyeballs, a trick that never failed. Until now. The leaders looked at him like this was the most boring thing in the world.

Big Bad Wongo looked especially unimpressed. He frowned and grunted hard, and all his eyeballs shot straight up into the air. They swooped around like a flock of small birds and then circled back down. Wongo simply tipped his head back, opened several of his mouths, and caught them on his tongues. He swallowed and blinked, and the eyeballs reemerged from his various eye sockets. Glyzix had always considered himself the master of crazy eyeball tricks, but now he sat back down in his chair—a little sad and a lot freaked out—unable to imagine anything he could do that would wow this crowd.

The aliens all stared at Freddy with pure hatred.

Wizbad chuckled. He was amused because it looked like the alien leaders would finish Freddy off even faster than he'd hoped. They were so fired up now, there was no way Freddy could recover. Wizbad decided it would be more fun to stop messing with the translator, sit back, and watch Freddy fail miserably on his own.

Freddy was definitely in trouble. He had to do something . . . but what? Then he had an idea. He held one finger in the air, cleared his throat, and spoke into the translator. "Ahem." He lifted his heaping plate of creepy-crawly appetizers, extending his pinky just so. "Pardon me, distinguished guests," he said in the fanciest fancy-dinner voice ever.

Glyzix looked at him like he was nuts. Was this really the time for a display of politeness and etiquette?

"Sophisticated gents such as yourselves might enjoy the sort of high-class diplomacy used by senators and presidents and all kinds of bigwigs back where I come from. It's a little something we call . . . FOOD FIGHT!"

Wizbad couldn't believe it. This was the best the boy genius could come up with?

Freddy grabbed a huge fistful of squirming hors d'oeuvres and pitched them as fast as he could at Deathsnail, who caught every single one of them in his mouth. One wormlike one dangled from his lip, and he quickly slurped it in like spaghetti. Then he just sat there looking angry. His eyes narrowed and he breathed bloodred sparks from his nostrils. Freddy was sure he had made a huge mistake.

Deathsnail's whole body started humming like an engine revving up and it sounded like the appetizers were flying around inside the curved passages of his shell. The noise got louder and louder until finally Deathsnail pursed his lips. His cheeks inflated like a balloon, and he sprayed the appetizers back out at supersonic speed.

Big Bad Wongo took many direct hits in his many faces.

"FOOD FIGHT!"
yelled Deathsnail.

"FOOD FIGHT!"
said all Big Bad
Wongo's mouths. He

wadded up the food into a disgusting ball
and hurled it with all his might at Chewtyke.

Chewtyke opened wide and caught
the ball in his teeth. He chewed very fast,
grinding the food like a garbage disposal.
He swallowed . . . and then threw his head
back and laughed hard. Deathsnail and Big
Bad Wongo laughed too, and Freddy
knew his hunch had been right:

recreational food warfare is a universal pleasure. What a relief.

Laughs and squeals filled the air as bizarre food bombs exploded and splatted all around the dining room. Everyone was having a blast . . . except Wizbad. Things were going well, which, for him, meant things were going very, very badly.

# 15
# RUBBED THE
# WRONG WAY

**M**eanwhile, deep in the kitchen, the alien cooks had scrubbed Freddy's family clean and were now preparing them for dinner.

"Thank goodness we're starting over," said Babette to her chef, still mistaking him for a beautician. "Flurbians are such fashion morons. Now . . . I have some suggestions."

The chef had no clue what Babette was

saying. But he didn't care. He simply tossed her into a large vat of something.

"Oh boy," she said. "Some kind of spa treatment!"

Mom and Dad were thrown in too. The chefs rubbed them with sauces and marinades.

"Ooooooo," said Mom. "Massage oils!"

"Ahhhhh," said Dad, "could you get my lower back?"

"Hey, I'm next,"

said Babette. "I've had a pain in my neck ever since I got to this stinking planet."

But instead of rubbing, her chef started pounding her with a meat tenderizing mallet.

"OUCH! OUCH! OUCH!" she screamed. In between ouches Babette noticed something. The massage oil smelled an awful lot like barbeque sauce.

"Wait a minute. WHAT'S GOING ON HERE?!" she shrieked.

That did it. The chefs were sick and tired of listening to the obnoxious whining of these annoying ingredients, so they shoved a Flurbian apple into each family member's mouth.

# 16

# FAMILY-STYLE DINING

**B**ack in the dining room, the party was in full swing. Freddy and Glyzix were on the table playing a strange version of baseball. Glyzix pitched flaming Flurbian vegetables at Freddy, who whacked them around the room with a gigantic wooden spork. The aliens got a kick out of catching them in their mouths, ears, noses, and eye sockets.

Wizbad drummed his fingers and looked at his watch. He was extremely irritated that Freddy's stupid antics were winning the alien leaders over. "WHEN WILL DINNER ARRIVE-ETH?!" screeched the evil wizard. "THE SERVICE AROUND HERE IS HORRENDOUS-ETH!"

Just then, the kitchen door flew open and Wizbad smiled. Six Flurbian guards carried three huge platters covered with gigantic lids. Freddy of course had no clue that his family members were under them.

"Finally!" he said, holding the translator

in his hand. "Now we can all give thanks for this bountiful feast we are about to chow down on! I am absolutely certain that these dishes will be scrumptious and mouth-watering and however you say 'scarf-o-licious' or 'yumtastic' in your languages."

Wizbad smiled a large, sly smile. "Do you pledge-eth, King Freddy, that you will eat everything on-eth your plate?"

"Sure do," said Freddy.

"Because," said Wizbad, "our guests are sensitive about this issue. It's very important to them."

"I know!" said Freddy. "I'm not finicky. I promise I'll devour every last bite. No more delay—let's eat!"

As he spoke, he gestured dramatically with his hands and accidentally let go of the translator, which crashed onto the table and exploded into pieces. Freddy wasn't concerned though, because everyone was getting along so well . . . and at this point the sharing of food was the only communication necessary. The aliens were incredibly hungry. They were salivating, slobbering, and lip licking

like crazy. Chewtyke was grinding his teeth so hard, the metal-on-metal sound was deafening.

A Flurbian guard snapped his fingers and toes and the lids on the dishes floated up into the air, revealing the monstrosities underneath. The room erupted into applause.

It took Freddy a second to recognize his family on the platters, and his mouth fell wide open. Mom, Dad, and Babette were alive, but there was some kind of glaze poured over them and Flurbian flies the size of pigeons were buzzing around. The fruit wedged in his family's mouths made it impossible for them to talk, but their faces told the story. Except for Babette. She was so thickly covered with marinades, sauces, and creepy-crawly seasonings, you couldn't even *see* her face.

Freddy wanted to scream, but he bit his

tongue. Since the alien leaders were hyper-sensitive about the whole food thing, this was probably not the time to upset them. On the other hand, he wasn't about to sit around watching his family get scarfed. He couldn't believe it. Somehow he had gotten them into deep trouble again. He looked at the smashed translator on the table and gulped.

# TASTES LIKE CHICKEN?

"Sheesh, Kingster," whispered Glyzix, "if I didn't know that was your family, I'd say they are the most delicious-looking meal I've ever seen."

"Thanks," said Freddy, "I'll be sure to pass on the compliment."

Freddy had to admit, the presentation *was* pretty amazing. The alien leaders stared at the spectacular dishes with their tongues hanging out. Several of Big Bad Wongo's tongues twisted around each other, and he salivated heavily.

Deathsnail looked at Freddy and signaled that it was time to serve. He frantically pointed to his wrist, then to the "food," then to his mouth: the universal signal for "HEY YOU! I'M STARVING HERE!"

# FROM HORRIBLY BAD
# TO HORRIBLY WORSE

*That's it*, thought Freddy. It was so simple, really. He would have to explain the situation through pantomime—a high-stakes game of charades.

Freddy leaped onto the table. He would have to communicate so clearly that he could not possibly be misunderstood. He must be polite but firm. If he came on too strong, the whole thing could spin out of control and any one of these alien leaders would wipe him out in two seconds. And then the family and probably the entire nation of Flurb would be helpless against them.

It was a simple message from the heart: "PLEASE, GENTLEMEN, DO NOT EAT MY FAMILY."

He held up his hands and wiggled seven fingers, showing that what he wanted to say was seven words long. Amazingly, the alien leaders actually seemed to understand. They each held up seven fingers and nodded their heads.

Freddy held up *one* finger: the universal gesture for "first word."

Deathsnail, Chewtyke, and Big Bad Wongo each held up a finger and nodded again.

Freddy got down on his knees, made a sad expression, and clasped his hands together like he was pleading or praying.

"PLEASE!" said Glyzix.

"PLEASE!" repeated Chewtyke, Death-snail, and Big Bad Wongo.

Amazing! Freddy was actually teaching them words! But how would he get across "gentlemen"? He looked at the horrible specimens seated around the table and decided to cut it to *six* words.

The next few were easy. Freddy shook his head for "DON'T!" and pretended to

eat for "EAT."

"DON'T EAT!" said Glyzix.

And they all repeated, "DON'T EAT!"

Freddy realized that "MY FAMILY" would be a lot harder. He acted out his parents meeting, falling in love, getting married, Babette and Freddy being born, all living together in their little house, Babette and Freddy fighting, everyone getting abducted by Flurbians, you know, family stuff. His performance was a masterpiece of pantomime.

"MY FAMILY!" squealed Glyzix.

"MY FAMILY!" said everyone else.

Everyone but Deathsnail. It turns out that "my family" sounds exactly like "you big fat idiot" in whatever language he speaks. So when Deathsnail put it all together he got: "PLEASE DON'T EAT, YOU BIG FAT IDIOT!"

Deathsnail turned to his little sluglike assistant. He grunted something that made the assistant stare intensely at Freddy and growl like a rabid dog . . . or at least like a rabid slug.

But Freddy wasn't worried. It was just a little slug! He laughed and talked in baby talk: "Whoa . . . what's the big, bad sluggy-wuggy gonna do now?"

A small door in the slug's forehead slid open and a huge, horrifying weapon telescoped from within his brain and stopped about an inch from Freddy's face.

"Oh," said Freddy.

The slug didn't say anything. He just blasted away.

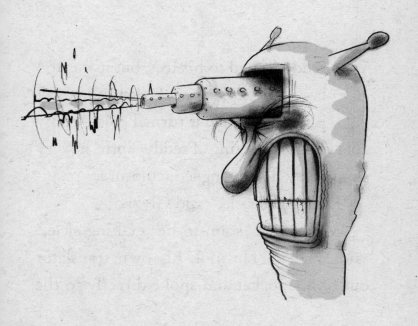

# 19
# A CHILLING DEVELOPMENT

Freddy leaped to his feet, but it was too late. An explosion of alien slime hit him hard. Then it turned cold—really cold—flash freezing Freddy into a very slimy, very disgusting ice sculpture.

"Holy king-sicle," said Glyzix.

"Make that soon-to-be *ex*-king-sicle," said Wizbad. He took his own translator out of his pocket and spoke directly to the

leaders. "HAIL-ETH FREDDY, DESSERT OF FLURB!"

"NO!" screamed Glyzix, but before he could leap to Freddy's aid, the Venomoids slithered around him, tying him tightly in knots.

"You can't save your precious king!" Twork laughed.

"You can't even save him for *dessert*," said Babs. "There's not enough to go around!"

Glyzix waited for the third Venomoid to chime in with his usual idiotic comment, but he didn't. Odd. "Where's Blif?" he asked.

"Umm, he left," said Babs. "He wasn't feeling well. He was nursing a paralyzed brain you know."

"IT'S . . . CHEW TIME!" shrieked Chewtyke, the words squawking from Wizbad's translator. He liked chewing a whole lot more than sitting around talking. He pointed to the figure completely covered with gloppy sauce. "THAT ONE LOOKS NICE AND CHEWABLE!"

He leaped into the air with his mouth wide open and ate Babette in two or three bites. Four tops.

Glyzix gasped in horror. Deathsnail and Big Bad Wongo also gasped,

but it was only because they were jealous that they hadn't thought to go first.

Freddy would have gasped, but he was frozen solid. He looked on helplessly. He had failed his big sister. Sure, they'd had their differences since the second he was born. She

had been kind of mean to him sometimes. Actually, lots of times. She hadn't even given him a birthday present. But he knew that he would miss her. Sometimes you don't appreciate people until they're gone.

And, boy, was Babette gone.

Chewtyke burped a long, satisfied belch . . . and sat back down to rest for a moment. "Hmm . . ." came his voice through the translator, "that dish was delightful but oddly light . . . not at all filling. . . . I think I'll have seconds."

# 20

# A PRICKLY, PORTLY SITUATION

**M**eanwhile, outside the palace, something was running down the middle of the street. This something was quite fat and prickly . . . like a porcupine crossed with a huge pig. The Flurbian passersby had never seen such a monstrosity. They dived out of the way and hid in alleys, shaking with fear. They watched in terror as the crazed porcupig

began tearing off its skin.

It was Babette. She had escaped in the kitchen, and Chewtyke had only eaten an empty Babette-shaped shell of hardened marinades and sauces. Since she was pretty sticky from this ordeal, anything she touched—sticks, stones, small Flurbian critters—had stuck to her, and now she tried desperately to shed them.

She was searching for an entrance to the underground canal system, hoping to locate the ship that had brought them to Flurb, so she could hightail it back to Earth.

"There seem to be entrances *everywhere* until you really *need* one!" she cried.

But no sooner did she say that than a friendly Flurbian child called out to her.

"Whatcha looking for, ugly porcupig person?"

She told him.

"Oh," he said, pulling a lever that looked a lot like the branch of a tree.

The ground opened up, and Babette fell through. "AHHHHHHH!" she screamed. This was exactly the kind of thing that Babette was really sick and tired of. But her mood quickly changed when she landed right on the dock they'd arrived at and saw that the ship was waiting.

All she had to do was plead with the ship to take her home. At this point, she just wanted to go back to Earth, even if it meant leaving her family behind. She convinced herself that Freddy could get her parents out of this mess just like he had every other time death and destruction knocked on the family's door. They would be all right . . . right?

# 21
# WORST BRAIN FREEZE EVER

**W**rong. Chewtyke was more than ready for another course. He started grinding and salivating at Mom and Dad.

This did not sit well with Deathsnail and Big Bad Wongo, who were planning on enjoying the rest of the family themselves. The three began arguing about how to divide up the feast.

Freddy watched all this in horror. He had to think! If only he could summon Orange Beauty . . . but he couldn't move a muscle. Wait! He had defrosted slightly and realized he could just barely move his left eyelid. Maybe he could wink a message to Glyzix, who could call for Orange Beauty! Freddy would wink to spell things out: one wink equals the letter "A," two winks equals "B," and so on. This would be hard and slow going, but it was worth a try. Sooner or later the alien leaders would stop arguing and chow down. Probably sooner.

Freddy determined that Orange Beauty's stable was three floors below and about forty feet to the left. He just had to get Orange Beauty (via Glyzix) to fly up and break through the floor beneath them, lifting the table up to the chandelier, so that its candles would melt the ice he was encased in, thus setting him free. No problem.

Freddy stared at Glyzix and got winking. He winked fast. Fast for a frozen eyelid, that is. And, unbelievably, Glyzix seemed to understand.

Meanwhile, Deathsnail, Big Bad Wongo, and Chewtyke had decided to draw straws to see who would get the first bite

of Freddy's mom and dad. But soon the alien leaders started fighting over the straws.

As his eyelid continued to thaw, Freddy winked faster. He winked like the wind! While winking, he noticed a small alien sitting at the table that he hadn't noticed before. This alien was unbelievably ugly. Freddy thought its nose was running, but then he realized the nose *itself* was dripping off its face. In fact, the entire face seemed to be sliding off its head. And the alien was winking back at Freddy.

Was it trying to tell *him* something? He didn't know. But he did know that it was now smiling *and* winking. And then it started smiling, winking, and *blowing kisses*! What? This disgusting little drippy-faced alien was flirting with Freddy? Barf-o-rama! Times a gazillion!

This whole thing was very distracting

and Freddy was
sure he would
lose track of
where he was in
spelling out the
message to Glyzix.
But somehow he
focused and finished,
and Glyzix nodded.
He'd gotten the
message.

Glyzix did a fast series of Bionic Belches and Gassy Whistles: *"BURRRRRR-EEP-EEP-EEP-BLAMMO-BLAMMO-EEP-EEP-BURRRRRR-EEP! TWEET-TWEET-ZZZZZOP-HOOTY-HOOT-KABOOM-BOOM!"*

And three rapid-fire screaming, yelling Big Fat Asteroids: *"KERRRRRRRRRRR-ZOINK-A-MA-BLAM! KERRRRRRR-*

*RRRR-ZOINK-A-MA-BLAM!*
*KERRRRRRRRRR-ZOINK-A-MA-*
*BLAM!"*

And then the Flurbian Flabberblaster:
*"ZIP-ZIP-FLABBO-FLABBO-*
*FLURBO-FLURBO-BOOM!!!"*

Freddy knew that in no time Orange Beauty would burst into the room and really throw her weight around.

# WHEREFORE ART THOU, ORANGE BEAUTY?

But nothing happened. This made no sense. Orange Beauty was a trusty steed. It wasn't like her to ignore a call to action. Was she still mad at Freddy for banishing her from the dining room?

Freddy regretted how he had treated her. How could he have been so disloyal to such a loyal friend?

He signaled Glyzix to repeat the message.

Glyzix started in again. But he was losing his voice. He had blown out his vocal cords with all those Bionic Belches and Gassy Whistles. He tried with all his might, but his voice was barely audible now. Orange Beauty couldn't possibly hear him.

23

# EVIL-ER AND EVIL-ER

At the other end of the table Wizbad had curled up in his chair like a creepy, contented cat, watching all this and smiling to himself. He was sure his wonderfully terrible dream of becoming king would soon come true. He knew that Glyzix's sore throat wasn't the problem. Orange Beauty couldn't hear him because she couldn't hear *anything*.

Wizbad had taken the liberty, when he had left the table to supposedly use the restroom, of inserting earplugs into the ears of the sleeping Orange Beauty. He remembered what had happened the last time Freddy summoned her, and he wasn't about to let that happen again.

Meanwhile, the alien leaders finally figured out a system for dividing up Mom and Dad for dinner . . . and Freddy for dessert.

Chewtyke was measuring the family, marking them up for dissection. Big Bad Wongo was sharpening a large laser carving knife. Deathsnail chanted into the translator: "WE WANNA EAT! WE WANNA EAT! WE WANNA EAT!"

# 24
# SOMETHING BIGGER THAN ONESELF

Orange Beauty was deep in slumber and having a wonderful dream. It was her favorite dream. She was flying along in the wide-open spaces of the Flurbian outback with Freddy hanging on for dear life and laughing uncontrollably. She was laughing too. She loved her life since Freddy arrived, even if he was stern with her sometimes.

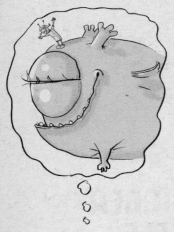

In the dream, Orange Beauty heard someone calling her far in the distance, but it wasn't Freddy. It wasn't Glyzix either. It wasn't even a dream. It was Babette.

Babette decided at the last minute that she couldn't abandon her family. She returned and peered into the dining room and realized what Freddy was trying to tell Orange Beauty through Glyzix. She ran down to the stable and screamed at Orange Beauty, desperately trying to relay the message herself. She did Bionic Belches and Gassy Whistles and Big Fat Asteroids. She even did a Flurbian Flabberblaster.

But Orange Beauty still did not wake up.

# 25

# A WHOLE LOTTA SHAKIN' GOIN' ON

"CARVE 'EM UP!" screeched Death-snail.

Freddy was shivering like mad. He was cold and scared, and that is

a very shaky combination. But then things got a whole lot shakier. The palace started to rumble. The chandeliers rattled, the bricks crumbled, and the entire world felt like it was going to explode.

*At last,* thought Freddy. Orange Beauty was finally here! She would break through the floor below him and lift the table up to the rafters, just as Freddy had planned!

The alien leaders, Mom, Dad, and Freddy all vibrated around the tabletop like the plastic players of an old-fashioned electric football game.*

Big Bad Wongo was shaking so violently, he couldn't keep the laser knife steady.

Wizbad leaped onto the table. He was angry, and telltale smoke and lava started streaming from his ears. "Give-eth me that!"

---

*Ask your parents.

he squealed, grabbing the knife. "I will do-eth the honors!" He smiled and stepped toward Mom and Dad, ready to attack.

Suddenly, Orange Beauty *did* come crashing up through the floor, sending stone and mortar flying and causing the palace itself to complain: "I am really getting sick of this! Just because I'm made of stone doesn't mean I don't have feelings!"

But there was still a problem: Orange Beauty missed the table by about an inch and a half. Freddy had made a small math error during all that winking.

Still, the huge orange steed flapped with unbelievable energy, her wings beating faster than a hummingbird's. The friction caused a lot of heat . . . and a hot wind swirled like a tornado around the dining room.

Babette hung on tight to Orange Beauty's leg . . . a pair of earplugs falling from her hand. She screamed, "Babette to the rescue!" but when she realized they had missed the table and were still heading skyward, she just plain screamed. Orange Beauty crashed through the roof and disappeared with Babette hanging on for dear life.

The vibration stopped. The dining room was now completely still. Wizbad smiled again, his horrible head surrounded by green smoke. He held the laser knife out in front of him like a sword and moved toward Mom and Dad, laughing diabolically.

Freddy felt helpless. He also felt *wet*. The hot wind from Orange Beauty's wings was melting the ice! He pushed against it as hard as he could from the inside, groaning and grunting with all his might, until the slimy ice exploded in all directions. Freddy was still shivering and possibly frostbitten but free at last—and uneaten.

Wizbad glared at Freddy. "I say we have-eth dessert first!" he cackled. He switched the laser knife's beam on and waved it way too close to Freddy's head, giving him a lop-sided haircut and blowing a gaping hole in the wall behind him.

Freddy dived and rolled across the table-top. He quickly untied Glyzix and then grabbed Twork and Babs by their tails and cracked them like whips. He let them fly and the snakes shot across the room and spooled around Wizbad's waist, knocking the laser knife out of his hand in the process. The knife's beam sliced through the encrusted sauces covering Mom and Dad, freeing them. The aliens looked on, flabbergasted.

"I think *this* delicacy need-eth a garnish," said Freddy, and Glyzix inserted all three apples into Wizbad's mouth.

Then Freddy yanked hard on the snake whip, causing Wizbad to spin like a top, fly off the table, and tumble down into the huge hole in the floor.

Freddy tossed Twork and Babs in next, and they landed on the defeated wizard's head.

"Ouch-eth," said Wizbad.

Freddy and the others bombarded Deathsnail, Chewtyke, Big Bad Wongo, and their assistants—using the remaining

bizarre garnishes and side dishes from the table's hidden compartments. What started out as a deadly serious battle quickly became one last round of their food fight, and pretty soon everyone was laughing and the dinner party came to a close. Even Mom and Dad joined in, seemingly unaware of how close they'd come to being feasted upon.

The aliens returned to their ships, declaring how impressed they were with this new boy king and his skillful, creative diplomacy. "TO MOLARIA!"

"TO WONGOLIA!"

"TO Z-9X G-VECTOR!"

"BUT WE RESERVE THE RIGHT TO RETURN AT SOME FUTURE DATE . . . TO EAT YOU! HA-HA! HA-HA-HA!"

"That was just a joke," Freddy said to Glyzix. "I think."

Flurbian citizens joined them in the courtyard, cheering, "HAIL, FREDDY, KING OF FLURB!" They laughed and even *danced* uncontrollably.

Wizbad had climbed out of the cellar. "I'LL GET-ETH

THAT MEASLY BOY KING YET!"
he howled at the two Venomoids perched
atop his noggin. But oddly enough, he was
quietly snickering to himself.

"Why's you laughing,
boss?" asked Babs.

"Yeah . . . what so
funny 'bout being a
total loser, boss?"
asked Twork.

# 26

# SUCCESS IS SWEET BUT SHORT

Orange Beauty had exited the Flurbian stratosphere before she even realized what had happened. She quickly returned and lowered Babette to the ground via her escalator tail. Freddy looked up at the huge, lovable orange monstrosity and made a series of bizarre clicks and sound effects that conveyed his deep appreciation.

Freddy and family had a group hug.

"What a fantastically fabulous king!" cheered Mom.

"I would have saved the day a lot quicker than you did if I hadn't been stuck in all that disgusting glop," said Dad. "But I have to admit, you're okay, kid."

"Babette wasn't bad either," said Freddy.

Babette looked at her brother. "Happy birthday, Freddy," she said.

Freddy was about to say thanks, but then he noticed that the ugly little flirting alien was still hanging around. It approached Freddy.

"Hello," it said. "Me love you, Freddy, King of Flurb."

In the interest of peace, Freddy thought he should let the pathetic creature down easy. "Sorry, not interested," he said, "but no hard feelings."

He reached to shake the alien's hand, but it wrapped its body around his like a snake. *Exactly* like a snake. It was the missing Venomoid in disguise.

"Hello, Freddy," said Blif. "I gotted you!" Blif, part machine of course, had been programmed for this by Wizbad.

Before Freddy's family knew what was

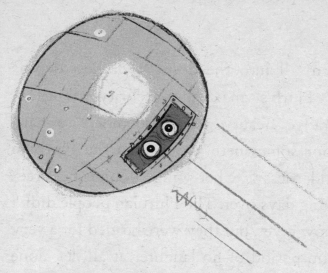

happening, Blif yanked Freddy to an await-
ing space pod, stuffed him in, and locked it
up tight.

It was cramped and uncomfortable, but
that wasn't the worst of it.

Wizbad removed the two Venomoids
from his head and aimed his wand at the
pod, blasting it into space. "The Freddy
is going-eth on a little vacation," he
cackled.

Then he ordered the Flurbian guards to
arrest Glyzix and Freddy's family and throw

them all into the deepest, darkest depths of Flurb's maximum-security dungeon. Orange Beauty was condemned to hard labor somewhere way out in the Flurbian wilderness . . . her wings bound, her free-flying days over. The Flurbian people didn't know it yet, but they were headed for a very grim period of no laughter at all, let alone the uncontrollable kind.

The seven Flurbian suns suddenly set, plunging the planet into darkness. It was just the end of the day, when the suns always set, but some-how it felt more final, like Flurb might be in dark-ness forever.

Everything had gone terribly wrong.

# 27
# CRUEL-EEPY GUYS FINISH FIRST

reddy, floating miles above Flurb, got a holographic phone call. Wizbad appeared before him, dried green lava encrusted about his ears. Wizbad leaned in close and laughed obnoxiously in Freddy's face.

"Well, the Freddy," said Wizbad, "my cruel-eepy dream has finally come-eth true. No big-eth mystery what that is . . .

just little old me being king and little old everyone else being slaves. Except for little old you. *You* have-eth the honor of floating aimlessly in your cramped and uncomfortable solitary confinement pod for—let me see—*ever*!"

"NOOOOOOOO!" screamed Freddy.

His shouting blasted through Wizbad's phone speakers and echoed throughout the kingdom of Flurb.

Glyzix, Babette, Mom, and Dad even heard it way down in the dungeon.

"NOOOOOOOOOOOOOOO!" they screamed in solidarity.

The Venomoids laughed the way evil lunatics do and then hissed in reply: "YESSSSSSSSSSSSSSS!"

To which Wizbad added, "ETH!!!!!"

The Venomoids slithered off to begin redecorating the royal chambers for their terrible, horrible, wicked, evil, immoral, dreadful, ghastly, and nasty new king. He had always been a pain in the nergzip . . . now he was a *royal* pain in the nergzip.

## 28

# IT'S NOT OVER TILL IT'S OVER, AND EVEN THEN IT'S NOT OVER

Freddy stared through the pod's tiny window into the vastness of space. It looked as empty as he felt. He had screwed up many times in his life but nothing like this. Not only had he let down his family, but an entire planet too! The pod rotated slightly, and Flurb came into view. Freddy reached into his pocket and found the little flashlight his parents had given him for his birthday. He aimed the light at the beautiful green orb below. He clicked it on and off, desperately trying to signal his family, Glyzix, and all of Flurb, using the same code he'd winked with earlier.

"Hello, all. I know it looks bad. Very bad. Horrible is more like it. And I don't have a clue how I'm gonna fix things . . . frankly it seems beyond impossible. Let's face it, it's gonna take a miracle. But if anyone down there can see this blinking light and decode this message—and that alone is highly unlikely—spread the word to all Flurbians who long to be free: I shall return to crush, clobber, whack, and whup Wizbad.

"Until then, your son, your brother, your friend, and humble leader . . . Freddy, King of Flurb."

# Don't miss Freddy's next adventure on Flurb!

# 1

# FREDDY, KING IN EXILE

"**G**ET ME OUT OF THIS FLYING SARDINE CAN OF DOOM!" howled King Freddy, pounding on the walls of his cramped jail pod, careening through deep space at ten times the speed of light. It seemed like about an hour since Wizbad had blasted

1

him off at the end of that horrible dinner party with Deathsnail, Chewtyke, and Big Bad Wongo, three of the most horrific alien leaders you'd ever want to not meet.

Soon after takeoff, he'd tried to communicate with his mom (Miriam), his dad (Al), his sister (Babette), and his best Flurbian friend (Glyzix) . . . blinking a message in code with his funky little Joe's Hardware flashlight. He hoped they'd received the message, but the truth was, Freddy didn't even know what had happened to them or where they were. Wizbad had taken them into custody and that no-good villain was capable of unspeakable horrors.

"ARRGH!" screamed Freddy.

He was a tad frustrated. "AAAAAAAR-RRRRRRRGGGGGGGGGGHHHHHHH-HHHHHHHHH!"

Make that a *lot* frustrated.

"Why me?" he wondered aloud. "Back on Earth, when teachers asked, 'Hey, Freddy! What do you wanna be when you grow up?' Did I say 'You know, I've always dreamed of being king of a distant planet, where an evil alien jerk with a magic wand sticking out of his head will constantly torment me and a bunch of killer alien dictators will nearly eat me and my family for dinner'? NO, I DID NOT!"

Freddy wondered why ex-king Wormola had selected him from everyone in the universe to rule Flurb. He wondered . . . but there was nothing he could do about it now. *The fact is, I am king and I promised to protect and serve Flurb and that's what I must do. Just as soon as I get the heck out of this space-traveling tomb.*

Freddy really had no clue how he was going to do that. And he had no idea where he was. Space is a big place.

# MESSAGE IN A BUBBLE

Just then, a light flickered in front of him. It blinked and buzzed and popped into a few weird shapes before finally taking the shape of Wizbad's head. His freakish features came into focus and floated there in front of Freddy. "Greetings, King. I mean-eth *used-to-be* king! I mean-eth *obviously-never-should-have-ever-been* king!" Wizbad cackled. His famous fang, which had broken

off during an earlier battle with Freddy, had been repaired and it was now twice as big and stupid looking as before.

"Listen, you worthless piece of space scum!" said Freddy. "Turn this tin can around and step on it!"

"No can do-eth," said Wizbad. "But what's the problem? You got an all-expenses-paid seven-billion-mile vacation out of this! And counting! There's enough fuel in that tank to hit the quadrillion-mile point. It gets amazing mileage. So you might as well relax and enjoy the trip, even though I intentionally designed this thing to be totally unenjoyable. No TV screen or magazine rack or books or games . . . pretty much nothing to do for the rest of your miserable life! But you're lucky compared to your beloved family."

"What have you done to them, you lunatic?!"

"Gosh," said Wizbad, "I'm glad-eth you asked."

Another light flickered next to Wizbad's head. It created a bubble, and in it appeared an out-of-focus hologram. As the scene sharpened, Freddy realized it was his mom, dad, Babette, and Glyzix. Freddy was happy to see his family again, even if they couldn't see him. They seemed to be engaged in some kind of physical activity, like a sport or something. Freddy couldn't quite make it out.

*At least they're out in the fresh air*, he thought.

But when everything came into focus, Freddy realized that his family and friend were swinging sledgehammers and breaking rocks in the hot Flurbian desert, shackled together in a chain gang.

# Don't miss any of Freddy's adventures in space!

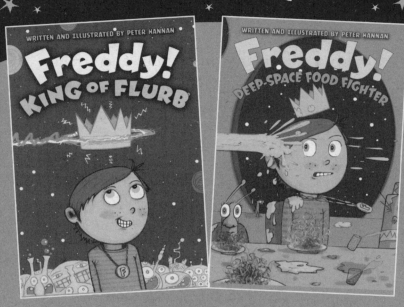

Freddy and his family have been abducted by aliens! Next stop, the planet Flurb, where things couldn't be more different from their ordinary life on Earth. On Flurb the aliens make Freddy KING and everyone worships him! Well, maybe not everyone. Not the vicious leaders of nearby planets, who want to publicly pulverize him, not his scheming sister, Babette, who can't stand being ruled by him, and certainly not the superjealous Wizbad, who will stop at nothing to knock Freddy from his throne!

## HARPER
*An Imprint of HarperCollinsPublishers*

www.harpercollinschildrens.com